Proof of a Tongue

POEMS BY

Sandra Alland

McGilligan Books

Library and Archives Canada Cataloguing in Publication

Alland, Sandra, 1973-
    Proof of a tongue : poems / by Sandra Alland.

ISBN 1-894692-08-X
    I. Title.

PS8551.L543P76 2004   C811'.6   C2004-904323-4

Printed in Canada

Excerpt from "Coal" by Audre Lorde from the book, *Coal,* published by W.W. Norton & Company, 1968, copyright estate of Audre Lorde. Excerpt from "When I Die" by Nikki Giovanni from the book, *My House,* published by William Morrow and Company, Inc., 1972, copyright Nikki Giovanni.

The author would like to thank the Ontario Arts Council and the Toronto Arts Council for their generous funding.

Editor: Stuart Ross
Copy editor: Noreen Shanahan
Cover photo: Sandra Alland
Cover design: Rodrigo Barreda
Inside design: Heather Guylar
Author photo: Sandra Alland

ONTARIO ARTS COUNCIL
CONSEIL DES ARTS DE L'ONTARIO

Canada Council
for the Arts

Conseil des Arts
du Canada

torontoartscouncil
An arm's length body of the City of Toronto

Some words live in my throat
breeding like adders. Others know sun
seeking like gypsies over my tongue
to explode through my lips
like young sparrows bursting from shell.

Audre Lorde, "Coal"

Contents

ONE:

All the Wrong Places

Rip Tide

My first memory
is of drowning in Mexico.

It could have been
a romantic story, if my
family hadn't been
such tourists.

Meltdown

This is a town
of serial killers
and suicide vistas.

Cries of *faggot*
echo off the dirty shore,
uttered in schoolyards,
at parties in the valley,
before too many jumps.

Towering mud
falls in mute conspiracy
with today's wingless visitor.
Down the bluff it shadows him,
aching equally for escape.

Its view across the water
is the nuclear power plant —
house to a stalker
less human,
bigger.

Fifteen

Those nights were heavy with snow.
I trudged through drifts,
like running in water, to you.

Pursued by shadows of rapists
who fucked around the corner,
I searched our garden.

My hands groped
in ice and frozen worms
under the rock where you hid the key.

I smelled of cigarettes,
Singapore slings, and the sadness
teenage girls can't name:
the freedom of age
wrestling the prison of flesh.

So I'd creep up the stairs.

I always saw you turn out the light,
heard you scramble from the window to bed.

I kept your secret vigil in my pocket,
like pepper spray.

Almost Catholic

No one remembers how to walk,
here where everything moves backward
or not at all

The boulevards are golf-course perfection
and evolution is still debated weekly

Hydrofields buzz with young love,
clandestine beneath radiation

The persistent proof of strip malls and drunk driving
almost makes me believe

Yet this church was graced by rock stars once:
Gowan crossed himself in a pew,
his blue hair electric power,
a surge of hope amid stagnation

Outside, a sign says: *Abortion stops a beating heart*

But remembering him,
it's impossible to muster the same despair

Brothers

The skateboard was red
transparent
shaped like a fish
and thin

I inherited it
from my brother
for five dollars
and some pain

Somehow I rode it
through the sewer system
without dying,
swimming on its back
in darkness,
diving over chasms
whose depths I couldn't look into

But heard,
as bits of me fell in below

You could see
the fish's bones;
the plastic glowed
in the dark,
like a relative's
lecherous stare

The bones said,
Sister, it's only flesh
You can always leave it behind

Division

She said:
You have to beat
an olive tree before
it'll bear fruit.

She was unnaturally
rooted, hooked up to
ventilator, heart monitor,
tubes to all orifices
(plus more they
had created).

I couldn't argue,
having seen on
ultrasound, in barium
radiation glow, what
they had picked from
between her legs;
having imagined it
in the flesh: dark,
pulpy and fibrous,
detaching soundlessly
when plucked.

She shrugged:
Amazing what grows
out of pain.

There

It's possible for a town
to visit a traveller,
when she's distracted
picking bugs from rice
and scorpions from shoes.

It's possible for a place
to enter the foreigner.

In such moments,
nation
floats soundless in the wind.

Paris, Texas

After the ill of El Paso,
of Mexicans stopped
just north of the border

You go no further than Wal-Mart, amigo.

after the leather-clad cowgirl
scowling in the diner
and the woman with the bruised face
who gave us this room,
I wonder why I've driven
thousands of miles
tired and dirty, scared of men
who notice how I look at you,
to get here

where some movie took place,
the lock is decoration,
and the door too has scars
from being kicked in

After the crosses on hills
and the purple-eyed woman
who apologized too much
for misplacing the key,
I can't figure out
why anywhere called Paris
would move me
to risk love for romance

Yet we sleep almost soundly,
even with sad guitar riffs
vibrating our bones

In the morning
we forget everything
as we run for the car —
your bra, toothpaste, the mayonnaise

and my pillow,
the one I brought
to ward off nightmares

Multiplication

I love him briefly
in the half-light of exhaust,
coins dropping from my fingers
to prove it.

Tomorrow
there will be four like him,
stiffening as water mains freeze.

If Hands Could Blush

She held my hand tightly,
fingers pleading   *wait for me.*
Wait for   *later on.*
So I worship the clock,
follow its hands
southward and steady,
thinking: *our boyfriends must pass.*

Kissing a lover's mouth,
salted and saturated with tears,
I hear my voice tell him:
        in another place   (maybe)
        in another time
which, translated, means:
        I'm waiting for someone,
        so please wait for me.   Or:
        I'm selfish and uncertain.

She'll come only after
I abandon my vigil,
then I'll search to find him gone.

Star-crossed somethings
and double-crossed loved ones;
two girls without courage
to touch palms in the sun.
Theft and deceit
are not in my nature,
yet I'm caught red-handed
in the bedroom again.

La musée de beaux arts, Montréal

1/

Old friends united briefly
in a cold city.

2/

Despite what some might say
about painting an entire canvas
one colour, I lost myself in the
depths of that blue, its currents
returning me to Costa Rica.

Broad brushstrokes of water
near the farm I once called home.

3/

Chalices and tabernacles,
remnants of Catholic conquerors,
also conquered in a city
where tongues still twist
awkwardly away from English.

We shouted the labels, laughing:

Tabernacle. Tabernac! Calice!

Giddy with words
our mothers once would have
scolded us for.

4/

The photograph
of the woman
with a mastectomy:
it pulled me, mystified
by survival, the blue scar
a strange and beautiful river
rushing across her chest.

I had no words for that woman,
didn't yet know what mutant cells
awaited us in Toronto and Scotland.
I had no words.

Except a whispered
Calice. Tabernac.

Room 403B

Outside my hospital window,
voices rustle in the grass (you smoke).
Though you can fly to the moon
to escape what they say,
I must remain,
grounded and fossilized.

And they say:
We'll stop your heart if you try to follow.

You have my blessing;
I've never been able to hold
the heaviness of grudges
in these thin arms.
Below you,
my ears ring with silence.
A blister frets on my elbow,
pus longing for release.
IV drip, drips,
a taunt for presuming health:

You can't go. Not today.

Between Wars

These Falstaff attempts
at bravery are eating
away at your pectorals.
Any more decay
and Charles Atlas will
weep in his Wheaties.

Rippling abdomen of
starvation, pumped up
shoulders of nicotine.

The blood runs thickly
between your ears, paving
freeways of oddity over
the lush banks of your
memory. My hand upon
your cupped groin feels
devoid.

After Jerusalem

She cradled my cracked spine,
kissed my bloodied eyes,
eased the thorns
from under my nails.

Then her tears expanded
into raging rivers,
and washed away all sand.

With weight like this,
to swim defies more gravity
than flight.

Flail Chest

Legislate as crime: dislocation.
Strain those contaminated through abdominal emptiness.
Avoid infection by unconscious social choking.

Impair circulation with routine seizures
(what gets around becomes familiar).
Miscarried responsibility burns all evidence.

Stroke to fainting amidst amputated sanity.
Arrest for inhalation and spontaneous abortion.
Attack self-poisonings with epileptic fervour.

Acceptable defects involve severe bleeding.
Punish discolouration via ingested hypothermia
(the comatose bite from various angles).

Fracture communication with external nomads.
Convulse on cue when squeegee focuses.
Summon shock at requests. Wound if necessary.

The rib cage is sensitive to repetitive blows.

A Kiss for the Riot Cop

Last night I kissed
a riot cop

or I would have
if I could've gotten over
the 10-metre wall
4 concrete barriers
fencesfencesfences
past rubber bullets
tear gas fumes
pepper spray
plastic shields
water cannons
masks horses pistols fists

But I did blow him a kiss,
and he felt it

I saw him flinch

Subtraction

When two galaxies collide,
one turns cannibal,
eating the other
in giant mouthfuls
of stars and planets.
Not out of cruelty
but compulsion;
a law of gravity.

Stripped down and
left floating with
only the most useless
moons and stardust,
does the universe
blame?

Bubble Suit

1/

I could analyze
the Doppler Shift
of your voice
if it weren't for
the variable of thin films
of space.

2/

Lately I've been
suiting myself up
beyond the limits of science
into a bubble
out of satellite range.

3/

The rainbows are startling,
the roundness a kick.

4/

Layer upon layer,
I don watery protection
impervious to sound waves
and falsely beating hearts.

5/

Nothing exists in a bubble.

6/

Padded up in a circle,
I avoid disappearances
and other such primitive
tricks of the ear.

Somewhere in Italy

There can be no
un-reading for those with
photographic memories.

Her breasts emblazoned
themselves in my brain,
small beneath her sweater,
and firmly against
my ideas of plot.

Familiar drowning in foreign waters.

She pleaded,
Do not ask me what I am
when all I had done
was loosen her tongue
without sound.

So we ended,
unformed characters
with climaxes
in all the wrong places.

Missing: 4

he was five
I was what you might call
a sister without law or maybe
common
we were always talking about
fairies and he would draw
mess your mind right up
Van Gogh Kahlo sandwiches
unbelievable art simply by
talking and breathing in so
intensely that his saliva would
make this hissing
the way air sounds
outside a plane window
jarring you out of comfort

carrying you far from home

Blue

I've never seen
trailer parks at dawn,
but I picture antennae
kissing the sky
like water witches
divining for Oprah.

I drive around the world
as if there were no dry spells,
yet near an ocean of icebergs,
I think of a desert sprawl
of moveable houses.

The Atlantic blows so cold
it turns the ice to blue.
H_2O and salt sea
make cacti seem ridiculous;
only in imagination
was the world ever warm.

Near Upala

Here the earth bleeds,
whether you cut it or not.
And it is cut.

And though my wounds
are clogged with it,
my feet stained red,
I cannot stop this bloodletting,
or the northern rain
that makes it flow.

Reasons to Stay #1

But the valley
is beautiful

But the valley
is beautiful

But the valley
is beautiful

Look there —
a fox is riding my skateboard

TWO:

Motion Muted

Flow

I have a memory
like the ocean;
everything thrown in
always washes up.

Only in a different order
and at the moon's discretion.

Nest

1/

Again, she said,
I've wasted too much time here.
as the clock ticked slowly
next to my swaying head.
And she had,
but I'd wasted more.

Her anger was too quiet
for her to hear it,
so she smiled,
made a cup of tea,
opened the newspaper,
pretended to read.
I hung over the bunk bed
like from a precipice,
the moment of decision
broken glass on my tongue.

Her mascara was running
again, black serpents coiling
around her breasts.
My tears always ran clear.

Poised to jump or speak
from my mattress mountain,
I studied the lines of her face
and couldn't move.

2/

She never glanced up;
it hurt her neck
to watch anything in flight.

That's why I started climbing:
I could study her better
as she sat unmoving for years,
Sears catalogue open on her lap.
I'd hang by my toes
from the chandelier,
awaiting the moment
she'd decide again
to leave.

Her eyes would flutter into focus
as she remembered her feet.
Then I'd turn on the radio
to distract her,
always with the same song:

If you were mine
I'd never let you leave me.

And she'd sit
and forget again,
motion muted.

3/

Climbing became an obsession.

One day I reached so high
she became a speck far below.
Toes propped up on a cloud,
I allowed my mind to wander
elsewhere.

But the birds would have their way,
forcing flight into my thoughts,
their wings flapping
like the pages of her catalogue.

My muscles resisted
descent,
so I invested in binoculars

and loved her from afar.

Hirsute

When follicles sprout on my surface,
friends don't call and relatives die.

Boxed

They left the casket top-half open
so we could say *goodbye.*
Some couldn't look,
some wailed, some glanced
and fled the room.

I waited, to be alone with you.

But your coffin was empty.
Grave-robbers all,
conspiracy of mourners
pretending you were there.

Checking over my shoulder,
I crawled in headfirst.
In the dark called a name.
Found only your nylons
and two calloused,
worn-down feet.

The Space

She showed me her palm
and said,
I'm a little person.

Then she began
to crawl inside me
to prove it.

Just let her try,
I thought,
not having noticed
I'd had a space her size
beneath my rib cage
for years.

Manicure

The night we
hung up on God
I'd already been
hung up on you
for light years of touch,
eons of phone calls,
an eternity of
electronic communication.

But we chose
in our new freedom
to speak for the first time
of death,
of rot and worms,
the pointlessness
of fingernails growing
in the grave.

Yours had caressed
my skin into welts
repeatedly, but I
contemplated them anew:

they were chipped and
yellow with years of
need, but in their
smallness spoke of growth.

I suddenly wanted in
you differently,
disarmed and soft,
deeper than claws can reach.

We Could Have Been in Love If It Weren't for Your Father's Dreadful Opposition to My Shoes

Lick my eye; feel what it is to see hope fade.

Cut

She and I owned razors early,
before we had hair in
those places.
The pink disposable kind,
with flowers
so we didn't get confused.

Each stroke,
each immersion in shaving cream,
drew blood
and paths through skin,
pink trails bringing us
somehow closer to
womanhood.

We'd stare at tampons
in awe, too.
Waiting.

They did come, of course,
the volcanic days when we bled
and grew hair everywhere,
even on our wrists.
Clumpy and shameful,
it interfered with romance.
A werewolf growl
beneath our best behaviour.

So we played Delilah
to ourselves, removing

our power, hiding
its feral resistance with bleach
and sweet-smelling soap.

I wore long sleeves even in
summer, but sometimes the
bandages showed,

and then their questions came,
hanging guiltily as she did,
later.
Always too late.

I stopped shaving,
but there are scars
where the hair
won't grow back.

Glass Collector

The smell of hospital
runs in my family,
a legacy of bruised veins
and renegade cells.

I trace my ancestors
along myriad paths,
but always to the same room.
The same nightstand
inherited across decades
with unchanging décor:

bottles for pills
bottles for urine
for blood

ashes

to drown in.

Naked and Clairvoyant

She met her lover at a strip club.
When he talked of Descartes
and Foucault,
she smiled warily:

All we got here's tits and ass.

He laid his hepatitis on the table,
told of his mother and retribution,
while she undid her bra strap,
felled him with a wink:

What's your sign?

He blushed as only voyeurs can,
his pretense all unfurled.
Yet she wasn't being coy:
her major was philosophy, but
she dabbled in astrology.

So she knew before he got there
that he was on the way.

Flood

At night, I become
his instrument.

While he sleeps.

Fingers moving to the
metronome of my breath,
he plays me.

The first to make a song
out of these exposed veins,
ready for the plucking.

Load

Your body weighs,
pulls love down
from inappropriate heights.

Such substance is a blessing:

to get a lover
fat as your own depths
to sink into gracefully
or not

to find a lover
wide as a 1000-year-old sequoia
    (brain like a tree
    sliced into rings
    This is where the damage occurred.)

I, too, am heavy
of heart,
and so cannot be moved
from you.

Addition

I never tell him
when he says
the same thing twice.
It's not that I'm
embarrassed for him,
repeating himself
like that, unaware.

I like the sound
of his voice

next to my skin,
vibrating through
molecules that find
the deepest,
untouched scars.

Each time is different
anyway, a sentence
dropped or rearranged,
inflection changed.
His lips form sound
with such miraculous
breath, it's hard
to believe he was ever
at a loss for words.

Ghost Pinch

Last night
the thought of you
raised a purple hickey
on my neck.

A little death
never hurt anyone,
but I'm wearing a scarf

just in case.

Hey Sammy, Yo Sammy

She calls *Hello!*
to Sisyphus
every morning.

The routine does little
to faze him.
Climbing upon her pedestal,
she waves.
But his hands are glued to rock.
She blinks twice,
lowers her head.

(*pause*)

Blood trickles off the pedestal,
down the mountain.

Song for an Execution

That woman's always out there knitting. Every time I come
here. Like she's waiting for the executions to begin. Is it a
scarf or a sweater for her dead son or does she undo it
every day and start again.

Maybe it's not the product that matters to her but the
process. Keeping her hands busy. That must've been
what it was like in France. Keep your hands busy so they
don't cover your eyes or maybe tear them out for being
there to see in the first place.

During the French Revolution crowds of knitting old ladies
gathered to watch the heads roll. Was it justice they were
watching for or boredom.

Did they make mistakes because their attention was
elsewhere, on blood and eyes still seeing after death.

Or were they good knitters who witnessed daily terror
without dropping a single stitch.

Up

We're all squinting at each other,
heads cocked, guns cocked,
all cocks sizing up the threat.

Up ahead the suspects.
Get out your swatches —
if they're darker than pink,
you're entitled to
paint them over
red.

Allah whispered fearfully
in alleyways.
Head coverings hidden
deep in closets,
illicit love letters to God.
Don't face the wrong direction
at sunset, brother.
I cannot be responsible.

We're looking daggers
at each other now.

The sky has opened up
on someone starving somewhere.
And the cry goes out:
Stand up, son. Be a man.
We want you. We want you.
We want.

Who was in those buildings?
Were they white capitalist
Christian soldiers all?
Were they barbarians, every one?
And those
And those

I cannot be responsible.
The scales of democracy
are on sale,
and the poor weigh too much.

Things were falling
from the sky that day,
things are falling now.
Unimaginable horrors,
but we won't look up.

We're looking sideways at each other.

Heavy

for Margaret Cho

What were those television executives doing
the moment your kidney collapsed

hatred filling your shrunken skin
hot racism stuffing your ears

Did they still plan it for some other girl
the next week   the next hour

Were they already writing her prescription
while you pissed blood in a cab somewhere

And in the miracle of your survival
what did they think of

Was it really money
or did they pray, begging on their knees

for something to take away your power,
their heaviness,
weights no diet can change

Ripe

Today I imagined
killing

the white woman who pushed
the black girl at the bus stop
the man yelling *slut* out his car window

years of violence
blossomed ugly
petals opening and falling
in rapid succession hatred

I saw flesh
collapse and slacken
grow purple
split.

Wandering Hands

touching was and still is and will always be the true
revolution
— Nikki Giovanni

In this impossible bed
of impossible sleep,
the possibilities of your hands:

how so small
how powerful
so electric
tender as memory

travelling my body so knowingly
I'd swear it wasn't their first journey
the night that it was

How did your fingers
caress the circumference of each vertebra
How did my nipples
recognize your palms through clothes
and centuries of separation

magician's hands without the sleight

hands with passport
free entry

tidal hands,
drawing all of me out onto the sheets by morning

and yet this ache

the fleeting possibility of their touch,
your impossibly beautiful hands

THREE:

Proof of Tongue

Lymphatic

At sixteen I had
my tonsils out —
couldn't talk for days,
my throat scarred,
my stomach bloated
with blood.

I liked it.

Quietly digesting
my own cells,
I was filled with
intimate knowledge

and no one asked me to explain.

Universal Larynx

When a woman opens her mouth,
the tides reverse.

When a woman opens her mouth,
earth shifts.

When a woman opens her mouth,
dogma cracks, tyrannies fall,
the stock market suffers a loss.

Boys drool.

When a woman opens her mouth,
someone turns up the music,
people avert their eyes from her face.

There is a howl of rage
and the snap of releasing bone.

When a woman opens her mouth,
women starve,
the word *sister* stuck in their throats.
A boy flinches.

When a woman opens her mouth,
men relax, girls feel safe,
there is plenty of water to drink.

Fear consumes her.

When a woman opens her mouth,
she sings or screams, bites or suckles,
destroys or lovingly soothes.

When a woman opens her mouth,
her lips shape language
I sometimes understand.

Shipwrecked

You don't look right, you say.
My silence paints discomfort
on your face.

I want to relax those lines,
blur your features with
proof of a tongue,
attempt a short phrase like:

I'm drowning in carcasses.

Instead I embrace you mute,
stroke histories into back muscle,
encode messages in
textured touch.

But your skin cannot absorb me,
so you leave without responding,

and I still haven't found
the words.

Love: 11

Breathless, I stumble
upon her naked.
(Diana killed for this.)

How to address
the undressed?

Her glistening skin
makes *good morning*
seem foolish, but

in the right position,
my tongue
could speak.

I Could've Been Famous If It Weren't for a Few Small Glitches

1/

Whenever they asked about love
I said yes

2/

Many Thursdays, it was food or rent

3/

I kept talking about women and calling them *genius*, which led to mass confusion rabid journalists thinking I had the gender wrong the name wrong the question the tense situation of explaining Toni isn't a man   indeed   a she billie neither   yes genius I said genius not genuine not German and not

that half-crazy isolated abusive icon of Western achievement male smart beyond their wildest masturbatory efforts able to memorize and spit out genius

Genius as in she who makes magic
and can also explain the trick

4/

pink orifices
sweet dilation

UN Translator

At the International Convention
the English frog said, "Ribbit ribbit, "
and the Spanish frog said, "Croac, croac,"
to which the Bulgarian frog replied,
"Qvac qvac. Qvac *qvac*."

Outraged, the Mayan frog yelled,
"Lec lec lec lec lec lec!"

The French frog stayed ominously silent.

In the Details

1/

In Russian and Bulgarian
the repetition of words
is considered sloppy.

You could never say:
"I saw Frank last week. After I said hello to him,
he accidentally stepped on my foot. All week I've
had a swollen foot because of Frank."

You'd have to say something like:
"I saw Frank last week. After I said hello to this man
who is my old friend, the tall male accidentally stepped
on one foot that is mine. All the past seven days, I've had
a swollen little part of my leg because of the guy I met
when we were both considering suicide."

I wish I spoke Russian or Bulgarian.

How else would I ever know
you were sad?

2/

In Bulgarian
there is no word for "ape."
"Ape" is "a monkey who looks like a man."
So you could never say,
"A monkey met an ape."
or
"A man met an ape."

This loophole
benefits the apes greatly,
because if they never meet any men
they can survive out there in the jungle
just a bit longer.

3/

Bulgarian has many more
past tenses than English.
The story is different
depending on whether or not
the teller was at the event.
Past retold, past experienced.

Bulgarians could revolutionize our encyclopedias
to say things like:
"The white man who published this book was told by some
other white men who read some other white man's diary that
the 'Indians' signed a treaty and therefore gave away their
land; however, as he was not actually at the signing, the
publisher's third-hand description may well be incorrect."

Of course without all that repetition of adjectives and
pronouns, but you get the point.

4/

Past retold:
My friend was sad and considered suicide.
I didn't receive a phone call.

5/

Past experienced:
I sat on the bridge and remembered everything.
I realized I am a monkey who looks like a man.

Tirer la langue

My francophone mother
failed French class
three times;
her tongue was stuck
to a pole in Cornwall
that someone dared her
to French kiss
in winter.

Good Stock

He never said much,
learned to suppress a language
that got him beaten
on both sides of the ocean.

He saved words for metal plates
and room-sized cameras,
measuring paper as if
clearing his throat.
(sentences formed
from photographs and fixer,
painstaking printing with
chemicals for tone)

Dinnae ask ays how Ah feel.

By osmosis I learned silence,
swallowed it like whiskey,
choked consonants with my uvula,
hid vowels behind my teeth.
Then placed words   carefully
on a page.

Books have an identifying smell,
like people; the world changes
when they open up.
This my father called *wirk*
and I call *breath*.

Every time I inhale one,
I know exactly what he meant.

Lost While Translating

There's this woman I'm reading.
No, that's not right.
There's a woman —
open like a book.
Still not it.
Her heart an ancient text.
My heart the devouring eyes.
No.

There's a woman,
she has words like no one,
sentences like never,
a woman I lost like a train
for a faraway land.
Not what I mean.

In English, you say,
What are you reading?
Rarely *who*.

There was a woman,
and I kept reading
what I'd been reading before.

Reasons to Stay #2

I learned Spanish
in grade 2
from Carlos
who taught me
his words for
land mine
and
blind

Nobody made fun
of Carlos;
we held his hand
tenderly at recess,
quietly mouthing
El Salvador libre
trying to understand
with small fingers
a fallout
beyond language

Feminist Fatale

1/

It's ridiculous to say
she lured me in —
to call her a seductress
seems sordid.
Really, her words
were the most rational
I'd ever heard.

2/

How truth tempts.

3/

She never once undid
her blouse while saying,

*Middle-class white women have a lot of
work to do if the women's movement is
ever to achieve any semblance of equality.*

nor spread her legs across my desk
with a sultry
Take up space because you can.

4/

Yet her mouth music
beckoned and caressed me,
promising fulfillment with a
consonant-clicking tongue.

Gender Thief

Sometimes
she dressed like a man
and snuck into
board meetings

Just to see
how things were done

We had sex
in parking lots
furtive
executive-style

I grabbed his tie
like a lifeline

my chance at umbilical

my clutch at need

Dreams of Kentucky

1/

In my dream
we're eating fried chicken
on a mountain in Nicaragua.
You peel the skin and
pass it to me gently, like treasure.
We don't comment on our
vegetarianism, nor the fact
that the meat is repulsive, that it
squishes strangely between our fingers,
like rubber or something rotten.
We eat.

Then we talk of times
when things were better. *Back then*.
I say, Things were better back then,
when I didn't notice my poverty,
when it didn't get between us,
painful as your desire.

We contemplate my poverty:
it jiggles on its frame
like awkward meat from a bird
that doesn't have real wings.

As always,
we ignore your desire.

2/

I'm with my mother
at the KFC in Orillia
when two bikers stop and stare.
One says, Hey didn't you take
pictures of that biker-hater.
I say, Yeah but he was a pervert.

The bikers smile
and place libations at our feet,
dabbing grease lovingly
from our fingers.

I look up and there's a cloud
shaped like Michael Ondaatje's chin.
I know then that Orillia's a good place,
despite its rapists and boredom.
I know boaters come there
not out of habit but longing;
we can all sense brilliance
dwelling among fast food chains.

Someone good will finally write a story,
my mother says as the better-looking biker
sucks on her thumb.

I hope she's a lesbian, I say to my mom,
the bikers, and Michael Ondaatje's chin.
For no reason really, it's a dream after all,
and in my dream my mother smiles.

Better yet, so do the bikers.

3/

In this one my ex-girlfriend shows up,
only she doesn't look like my
ex-girlfriend. She looks like one of those
leather-clad women from a sci-fi movie.
Well, she looks like my ex-girlfriend in that
she has my ex-girlfriend's face and body,
it's just that she's wearing this outfit
my ex-girlfriend wouldn't be caught dead in.
My ex-girlfriend is an ecologist.

Anyway we're at the KFC in Kingston;
we're on our way to Montreal and
she doesn't speak French but she's
pretending to, and people are buying it.
She says, Juh me lovay ce chickenois,
as she downs a drumstick in one swallow.
The crowd goes wild, but I'm not really
into it. I've seen this trick before, I think,
scanning the chicken-eaters for an escape
route. Luckily, my mother is waiting for us
in her car, so I grab my ex-girlfriend's
hand and make a break for it.

Vous ett le jumbo wingay, she screams.

I decide maybe it isn't such a good idea
to leave a scientist alone to think for too long.
But she does look good in leather.
My mother says so too,
but then she turns into Michael Ondaatje
and we don't have much
to say to each other
because we've barely met.

So we drop Mom/Michael
at the KFC in Oka.

Then my ex-girlfriend is suddenly
swimming in the ocean and
she's not wearing leather anymore.

4/

They have a KFC in Bermuda,
which may not seem weird,
except Bermuda has a law against
fast food chains, and is one of the
only places you can go that
doesn't have golden arches.

In this dream we're there,
you and I,
but we aren't eating anything.
We're staring at the Colonel,
wondering, What is he colonel of —
could we maybe call him *comrade*
or *hermano*. You say, Not bloody likely,
which is odd because you don't say
words like bloody, but then my
ex-girlfriend is kind of English so it's
probably her influence.

I say, He looks suspiciously like a contra.
You say, Be careful what you put in writing
or someone might sue you.
I say, What about freedom of speech,
but we're in Bermuda, a conservative place.

Then my mother shows up again,
only she doesn't look like my mother;
she looks like Fidel Castro.

I tell her, Wrong island, Mom, but
she's staring at you angrily, so
I decide not to mess with her right then.

You look upset, like we're talking about
something we shouldn't, like you're
wearing your underwear outside
your clothes. And then of course,
because I think it, you are,
and the Colonel starts laughing
at your underwear, and all the
chicken-eaters do too.
Suddenly my mother isn't so
angry anymore, at least not at you.

She grabs the Colonel and
punches him in the nose
and all I can make out is
Recipe for disaster that's what
repeated over and over.
She's stronger than Fidel should be.
But then so is Fidel.

That's when I realize it's really me
who's angry at you, for wanting to sleep
with your best friend. But what a stupid
thing to be angry over — who can help
desire anyway.

Next my ex-girlfriend shows up,
she's a Scorpio so she's never far
behind the word desire. And I ask,
But what does it all mean, and what
happened to Michael.

She grins and says,
It's like trying to figure out
what's in the chicken when
you don't eat meat.

5/

The last dream
is the best one,
but then dreams
of water always are:

I'm waiting to dock
in a village where
deep fry
can't be translated.

Acknowledgements

This book is dedicated to my grandfather, Isaac Alland (1912-2001)

Thanks & Love Brenda & Donald Alland, Megan Somerville, Stumblin' Tongues (esp. Andra Simons & Garth Kien), bill bissett, Corrina Hodgson, Alexandra Leggat, Jennifer LoveGrove, Goldy Notay, Jorge Lara Rivera, Stuart Ross, Marnie Woodrow, Susy Alvarez, Rodrigo Barreda, Patricia Boyle, Andrea Griffith, Reva Katz, Sasha Kiessling, Kerry Kuebeck, Jill Martingale, Elizabeth MacCormack, Michael McLeod, Michelle Ramsay, Tamara Toledo, Dory Turner, Nafsika Vlassis, d'bi.young, Zoe Whittall & Ann Decter of McGilligan Books, Shelagh Rowan-Legg of 13th Tiger Press, Women's Press, & the many others who have shown me support & random acts of kindness. Thanks to the radio & reading series organizers who let me do my thing, especially Ryan Ayukawa, Clara Blackwood, Allan Briesmaster, & Coman Poon.

Certain poems have appeared in some form or another in the following publications:
The Common Sky: Canadian Writers Against the War (Three Squares Press), *Resist!* (Fernwood Publishing), *Primitive Bubble And* (Proper Tales Press), *Aware in This* (Flow Sundays), *Fifteen Minutes* (13th Tiger Press), *The Mathematics of Love* (13th Tiger Press), *The Big-Eyed Love Child of the Instant Anthology, Dreams of Kentucky* (sandraslittlebookshop), *Partings* (Stumblin' Tongues), *Black Cat 115, dig., The Café Review, The Hinterland, ink, The Lazy Writer, Navegaciones zur, SEEDS, Tessera, This Magazine, Unarmed Poetry Journal, unherd, Who Torched Rancho Diablo?, The Writing Space*

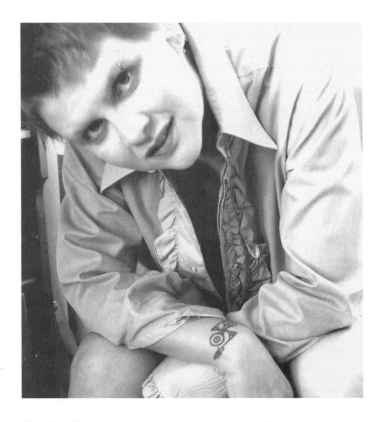

Sandra Alland was raised in Scarborough by two Scots and an anglophone French Canadian. She's a writer, performer, photographer, and small press fanatic. She has also been known to edit, translate, curate, and agitate. Her work has been published and presented in Canada, Mexico, Bermuda, Spain, and the United States. Some highlights include *Anything That Moves, Canadian Woman Studies, dig., Fireweed, Prism, This Magazine, The Common Sky: Canadian Writers Against the War* (Three Squares Press), *Resist!* (Fernwood Books), Hysteria: A Festival of Women, and Cheap Queers. At 2pm on the fourth Tuesday of every month, Sandra hosts In Other Words on CKLN 88.1. Recently, she was curator of the literary components of The Salvador Allende Arts Festival for Peace and Artscape's Queen West Art Crawl. *Proof of a Tongue* is her first full-length collection of poetry.